Caveman Farts

The Story of the First Stinky Fart

J. B. O'Neil

Published by J.J. Fast Publishing LLC

Caveman Farts

The Story of the First Stinky Fart

Table of Contents

For my son Joe, who loves to laugh about completely disgusting stuff like boogers, farts, Dutch ovens, wet willies, skid marks, ETC...Enjoy

FREE BONUS – Caveman Farts Audiobook!

Hey gang...If you'd like to listen to an audiobook version of "Caveman Farts" while you follow along with this book, you can download it for free for a limited time by going online and copying this link: http://funnyfarts.net/caveman

Enjoy!

The Best School Lunch Ever?

No doubt about it...franks & beans was Milo's favorite hot lunch of all time at school. Of course, chili-cheese dogs were pretty good and stinky...and corned beef and cabbage was fart-alicious, too...good old egg salad sandwiches always seemed to leave him in a good mood for the rest of the day.

But franks & beans was the definition of lunchtime awesomeness! Besides, what else was there to eat?

Mushy broccoli bits? Blech...

Carrot sticks? He cared-NOT for those!

Fruit cup? Forget about it.

Greek yogurt? Milo hated that worst of all. It made him fart LESS!

Milo wondered if all that gross food came from a gross-food factory. It had to. Did they really think kids would eat that stuff? Heck, Milo had never even seen *teachers* eat those horrible lunch items.

Milo mashed all the gross, unwanted food into a big, sticky, confetti-colored pile, then pretended to upchuck it all up onto the floor. That was a little funny, but not as funny as farts. Milo got up to get another big helping of franks & beans from Mrs. Boogerbottom, the lunchlady. He sat back at his table, lifted up a big forkful, and...

Brrrinngggg!

The lunch bell! Milo had no time to waste! He started chomping on franks & beans so fast that bits of food sprayed all around like woodchips flying off a power saw! All the kids passing by got covered in Milo's lunch, but before they could whine and complain, Milo launched a rocket-powered fart to get to class on time!

History Class + Mr. Stinkowitz = BORING!

Milo always had History class right after lunch, which was boring enough already without Mr. Stinkowitz rattling on and on about the origins of man and these hairy little Neanderthal cavemen. Blah blah blah blah blah...BORING!

Of course, Mr. Stinkowitz never talked about the really interesting stuff. For instance, Milo always wanted to know how the cave people went to the bathroom without any toilet paper. And where did they go? Did they sit on a log in the middle of the jungle with the dinosaurs and saber-toothed tigers walking around, waiting for them to finish so that they could eat the squishy little people? And of course the more he thought about all these important questions, the sleepier he got, especially with that big pile of franks and beans swimming around inside his belly...

Milo couldn't help it, but History class always seemed to turn into a farty naptime right after lunch...and as his head slowly touched his desk in the back row of Mr. Stinkowitz' History class, he drifted off to sleep thinking about farts...and cavemen...and farts...and cavemen...zzzzzzz...pffftttt...

Milo Dreams of the First Stinky Fart

Zug was a cave boy who didn't like to follow the rules. He thought rules were STUPID — he couldn't wait to be a grown-up Neanderthal so he didn't have to follow rules ever again. Just yesterday, he put a rock on his baby brother's head and tried to knock it off by throwing a bigger rock at it. They were cave-boys after all, and all they had to play with were rocks. Of course, his stupid brother moved his stupid head and the big rock hit him right in his stupid eye.

His mom grounded him for that, so he was stuck in the stupid cave all day. At least his pet dinosaur was there. His dinosaur, Dino, got in as much trouble as Zug did. Everyone else in his clan was super boring and didn't know how to have fun. Zug thought that maybe him and Dino could play a quick game of bite-the-rock-really-hard, but then he remembered that his mom had taken all the rocks away. He watched the cave paintings instead: there was a really good one in the corner that was his favorite.

It was getting close to lunchtime, and Zug started to feel really hungry. "Dino! Me Hungry! Find eats!" Zug grunted. Dino left to get him some food, and came back much faster than usual carrying a weird bunch of purple berries. He nudged some berries toward Zug, and Zug ate them up in one huge bite.

BURP! Zug thought the berries tasted pretty good. He'd never seen berries like them before. He wondered where Dino had gotten them.

Uh oh...

Zug's Belly Started to Rumble...

Zug's belly started to rumble. He could feel the pressure was building up in his belly like a giant bubble. He'd never felt anything like it before.

Zug jumped up and down, hoping that would help him feel better...but it didn't. He started running around the cave like his fur was on fire! That didn't help either. "What Dino do!? Zug no want to explode!" Zug cried. Dino did not seem as concerned as Zug would have liked.

Zug ran out of the cave, trying to find his mom. She was nowhere to be found. The trouble in his tummy grew bigger and bigger. His cheeks started to puff out. Zug was ready to pop! In a panic, he waddled as fast as he could into the woods.

Then it Got Worse...Much Worse

The rumble got worse and worse as he walked. He could tell that this was not going to end well. And just when he thought the bubble in his belly couldn't get any bigger, it did. It got bigger, and bigger, and bigger. Zug started to feel the pressure lessen in his belly and head, but now it was all in his butt!

His thoughts raced around, trying to figure out what was happening. No one in his tribe had ever felt anything like it, he was sure of that. If only he could talk to his mom...but she was way too mad at him. There was nothing to do but keep walking to the woods to hide so he could get rid of whatever this thing was building up in his butt.

It was getting really hard to waddle-walk. In fact, Zug started to walk on tiptoe, clenching his butt cheeks together as hard as he could.. That belly bubble was massive! In fact, he felt like it had nowhere to go but...OUT. Zug tried to squeeze his butt closed with his hands, and even sat on them, clenching his eyes shut. His whole body trembled!

But Zug reached his limit, and it was the most important event in the history of everything...

The First Butt Explosion!

Suddenly, there was no stopping it. The bubble EXPLODED out of his butt with a huge sound and horrible smell. CRACK! His butt-thunder launched Zug up from his squat, making him fall on his face!

He tried to sit up, but his fart pushed his head into the ground so hard his nose tore up the grass! Then lots of little farts fired out like machine-gun bullets, so fast and hard that they scooted Zug forward with every one! Pop pop pop pop pop pop pop pop pop!

When it was finally over, Zug pulled his head out of the ground and saw that he had made a trench almost ten feet long in the ground. He looked up in the sky and saw a big green cloud floating there. Zug dusted himself off. He felt fine. Better than fine!

He felt awesome!

"Zug has wind inside him!" He cried. "Zug found wind-berries!" He was sure this made him the coolest cave boy on the planet! And he knew that his mom was going to be really proud of him, even though he was still grounded for hitting his brother in the eye with a rock.

He couldn't wait to tell the rest of the cave people what had happened. He wondered if they were going to declare him the new Leader of the Tribe because of his amazing discovery, instead of that old guy with all the hair on his back. They were all going to be so happy!

Sadly, No One Seemed Happy For Zug...

Zug had a big smile on his face until he realized that all the women were running out of their caves, screaming! Zug was confused and worried. Was it an attack by their rival tribe, the Grunts?

Then he noticed that the men were running back from the fields where they were hunting. They never did that, and they looked really worried. Zug was sure it was an attack! He had to find his club!

“Zug! Zug, get club! Stupid Grunts make big big noise, scare everybody! Smash Grunts!” cried one Zug’s tribe mates.

Suddenly Zug realized what had happened. His bursting wind had spooked the tribe! Zug felt relieved, because now he could clear everything up, and everything would be OK!

Everything's Definitely Not O.K.

Then Zug saw the huge green cloud dropping down over the tribe. It was the stuff that shot out of Zug's butt, and it was getting lower and lower. Finally the cloud got so low that it covered the cave people, and they all shouted "PEE-YOO!" It was super stinky!

Zug was surprised, then horrified, because his tribe started to faint from the stinky cloud! Zug's stinky cloud! Suddenly Zug thought that maybe the wind he'd launched out of his butt wasn't so great after all...

“This no cave people doing! What make this terrible, stinky, stupid cloud!?” The still-conscious cave people demanded. Zug decided he didn’t want to take the rap for this, so he performed a second great historical action...

Zug Blames a Fart on His Pet

"Me know! Dino did it! Dino made big sound and green cloud after eating weird purple berries!" The tribe glared at Dino. Zug felt pretty slick, but he was about to get a big surprise. While Zug had been freaking out earlier, Dino really HAD eaten some berries...even more than Zug had!

Now here's the thing: dinosaur stomachs can handle a LOT more than Neanderthal stomachs, so Dino hadn't let his fart loose yet. But it was going to happen soon, and brontosaur farts were 10 times as powerful as caveman farts. In fact, as Zug pointed at Dino, he could see that something was very wrong with him. He'd never seen Dino look like this. His dinosaur cheeks puffed up and his eyeballs started to cross. Dino was rolling on the ground holding his belly. Then the pet dinosaur got up again, stuck his tongue out of the side of his mouth, raised his spiky tail all the way up in the air...and...

Can You Say...Dinosaur Farts?

As the entire tribe watched in disbelief, Dino suddenly let loose a deafening dinosaur fart that shook the walls of the cave! It was so powerful that small rocks -- and then big boulders -- started rolling down the sides of the cave, sending the members of Zug's tribe running for cover. "Big wind! Big wind come from dinosaur butt! RUN!"

This all took place so quickly that Zug was still pointing to Dino as the farting culprit. But his secret couldn't stay hidden for long, because Zug soon felt another huge bubble building in his belly making its way down from his stomach to his butt from the same fart-berries that Dino had given him...the berries that they had BOTH eaten!

Zug knew that if he wanted to protect the members of his stupid tribe, he would have to act quickly and heroically!

There was only one solution...

The First Underwater Fart Bubble...

Zug could tell his next butt bubble was going to be even worse than the first horrible fart that got him into so much trouble in the first place. He could feel it gurgling and burbling and churning in his body, quickly making its way towards its final destination: right out his butt! His tribe's homes couldn't survive another earth-rumbling fart!

So Zug did the only thing that he could think of to do – he ran away as fast as he could and jumped into the muddy pond next to his cave.

Because there was no way a giant, wet butt bubble would make any noise or smell at all if he jumped in the pond — right? Zug hoped that he would be totally safe farting underwater, and he felt good that his tribe would be safe thanks to his sacrifice...and so he JUMPED into the muddy water hole!

This Time, it Was Even More Awesome...

Just as soon as he splashed down into the water, that fart-berry butt bubble made its way down his belly, through his butt, and out the other side!

And what happened next was a surprise!

As the underwater stink-bubble was released from between his butt cheeks, it floated slowly to the surface. It seemed to get bigger and bigger as it rose silently in the water. And as this fart bubble reached the surface of the pond it erupted into a huge terrifying sound that sounded something like "Bloorp!"

And then there was complete silence.

Zug was stunned. He looked around at the rest of his tribe, who had all gathered around. The rest of the cave people were looking at each other wondering exactly what had just happened. They looked at Zug laying in the stinky mud, and he looked at them. And then they raised their caveman clubs in the air and started cheering! "Zug save tribe! Yay Zug!"

Once he came to his senses, Zug figured that his new underwater berry-fart discovery pretty much made him the coolest cave boy on the planet!

Zug Becomes the Coolest Farting Cave Boy

The cave people in Zug's tribe started to run towards the pond to get a closer look and smell at this crazy caveman miracle. Even the big hairy Leader of the Tribe walked closer to Zug to investigate. He got there just as Zug was letting off two more very cool underwater farts. "Blurp! Blurp!" Zug looked up at the Leader of the Tribe, wondering what he was going to say about this awesome new power of his.

The Tribe Leader looked up at Zug and smiled, even though it still smelled like rotten cave rats to stand this close to Zug.

"Zug," he said, "You and Dino make big green wind, and big water bubbles. We must control wind! How Zug make wind?"

Zug answered, "Zug ate berries, Dino ate berries. Berries make big bubble in belly, then make BIG wind out butt!"

The Tribe Leader turned to the rest of the cavemen and cavewomen, raised his arms in the air, and declared: "Zug have big strong butt!" The tribe roared their approval.

"Zug, you have big power," said the leader. "But call big butt wind not sound so good. Does not roll off tongue. Bad for posterity. Zug give good name to big butt wind."

Zug was beaming with pride – this was the best day of his life! He thought long and hard about what he should call it...until the perfect name popped into his head. It was a combination of the first little "ffft", followed by the big "BLART!!" he had heard. "Zug say it FART!"

"Fart." the Leader said quietly. Then he turned to the tribe. "ZUG MAKE FART! BIG BUTT WIND FART!". Then they all started cheering "ZUG FART! ZUG FART! ZUG FART!"

Zug had never heard people chanting his name. This was a dream come true. He wondered if he could use his amazing new farting powers to help the tribe somehow, instead of just making them pass out from the horrible smell. Zug turned to the Leader of the Tribe and asked, “How Zug use fart to help tribe, instead of make tribe scream and faint and run around like they crazy?”

The Leader replied, “If whole tribe fart, then no one scared of fart. You show me how to fart!”

Zug's a Hero!

So, Zug ran to Dino's berry stash and gave the Leader some of the same berries that he had eaten. The Leader cautiously looked at the handful of fart-berries. He smelled them. Then he stuck his tongue out and licked them. He seemed nervous.

The leader put the berries in his mouth, chewed them up, and swallowed them all. And then he waited.

But he didn't have to wait very long! Because almost instantly the Leader of the Tribe started to feel something building up in his belly, which was making loud “blurping” sounds. “Zug! Butt about to break! How stop!?” Zug began to laugh, remembering how he had first felt. “It ok Leader, you spread butt cheeks REALLY wide and let fart free!”

Then the Leader of the Tribe bent over, pointed his butt at the tribe, and then let out a smelly booming fart of his own. It was so loud that Zug’s ears were ringing.

The tribe covered their noses and their eyes started watering. And then they let out a big cheer for the Leader’s first fart! Hooray!

Everybody Learns How to Fart

"Farting easy. Farting fun! Everybody fart!" The Leader declared, and he and Zug passed out the fart berries to everyone. Soon the whole tribe was scooting around on farts, making plants wilt and sending big predators stampeding away.

"Now listen!" The Leader shouted. Everyone grew silent.

"Mean Grunts want to attack us again tomorrow. We tired of being bullied! We always peaceful tribe that no want to hurt anybody, but they make us mad and hit stuff! We use farts to end war! Make Grunts stop fighting!"

The tribe began to cheer. Then the leader pointed to Zug. "Zug, you must lead tribe to bring farts to Grunts! Zug tribe's only hope!"

"Hail Zug! Hail Zug! Hail Zug!" The tribe chanted.

Zug Was Feeling Really Good About Himself

This was turning out great. Zug was really excited to lead his tribe to victory over the Grunts! He felt so good that he let out his biggest fart yet, and it launched him off the rock he was sitting on and flipped him forward, right onto his feet!

“Ooh! Zug best farter in tribe!” One of the cavemen declared.

“Zug so dreamy...” the young cavewomen sighed together, and they crowded around Zug to get private fart lessons.

“Zug will teach everyone to fart best, but first we go to Grunts and stop war! Everybody follow Zug!” The tribe cheered and marched behind Zug as he led them across the Great Plains in the direction of the Grunt’s caves. They had a bit of a walk, but Zug had to find more fart-berries for their plan to succeed!

The Tribe Gets Pumped

Everyone was really excited now -- especially Zug's mom! She was so proud that her boy was now the tribe's hero.

As the tribe marched, Zug had Dino lead them to where he found the fart-berries. Dino sniffed like a dog until he led the tribe to a big tree with lots and lots of purple berries. The tribe took all the berries, which is too bad: it was the only tree like it in the world. That's why there are no more fart-berry trees!

The tribe munched on the berries and grew fartier and fartier. Soon they were trailing an ominous cloud behind them, and they chanted a battle cry:

"Grunts fear farts! Grunts fear butts! Grunts fear butts!"

Don't Mess With Neanderthal Farts

The Grunts were very surprised, and even though they were carrying big, vicious clubs, they were not ready for what happened next.

Everyone in Zug's tribe suddenly farted huge, horrible farts all at once, right at the Grunt's cave entrances The combination was so putrid, so foul, and so LOUD that the enemy tribe instantly fell on the ground and started crying.

“Stinky green wind! We no can smash wind! Stop, stop!” The Grunts cried, but Zug’s tribe was just getting started.

The Greatest Fart of All

The Grunts started to faint from the stink of Zug's tribe, but the tribes people's farts were starting to fade away. They had not eaten most of the berries.

Zug's tribe had one last secret weapon....Zug! Zug had eaten more berries than anyone, and his powerful butt cheeks strained to blast out the fart to end all farts!

Zug held on to a boulder to steady himself, and then slowly bent over to face the rest of the enemy tribe that was somehow still standing. He closed his eyes and held his nose, and then screamed “Me Zug! Me greatest warrior in tribe! Grunts never attack Zug and his tribe again, or we fart so hard you fly into sky! This only warning!”

And he proceeded to release the biggest and most powerful fart that the world had ever known. It came out so hard that it caught on fire! Scientists would later determine that this was the day that all of the dinosaurs disappeared from the face of the planet (and of course that’s why they refer to it “ex-stink-tion”).

Zug's Butt Saves the Day!

The mighty fart that changed the course of history sent the Grunts screaming into the sunset, never to be seen again.

Everyone in Zug's tribe was so happy. They would always be safe as long as they could perfect their use of farts!

The farting didn't end there, of course. They all continued farting as they hugged and cheered. Some of them turned their backs to send one last parting fart toward the fleeing enemy.

And as they turned around to march back to their cave, the members of Zug's tribe didn't even notice that their dumb-looking Neanderthal eyebrows and all the hair on their backs had burned off because of Zug's last fiery fart bomb. Scientists would later identify this moment in history as a very important day in the Origin of Man. In fact, even the most boring history teachers in the future would hang pictures of Zug on their classroom walls, and teach their students how important it is to fart every day, especially in the back row of the class...

Back to Reality With Mr. Stinkowitz

Brrrinngggg!

The bell for the next class went off, and Milo was so surprised that he literally jumped out of his seat. When he landed back in his chair he let out a lonnnnng fart. A *really* long fart, and it smelled like hot dogs and baked beans!

All the other kids started running out of the classroom, but Mr. Stinkowitz just stared at Milo looking like his head was going to explode. Boy was he mad...and he let Milo know it.

"Mr. Snotrocket...it's bad enough that you have absolutely no interest in learning about the Origin of Man on this planet. It's bad enough that you fall asleep in the middle of class snoring and farting. But ripping a monster fart in my classroom is completely disruptive and disgusting. You've got detention Mister! I'll see you right here in this classroom after school today!"

"But Mr. Stinkowitz, I learned so much today! I learned about the first cave people, and how they discovered farting by eating berries that don't exist anymore, which really stinks because those would be super cool! And I learned that the dinosaurs vanished because of a fart, and that farting evolved Neanderthals into humans!"

"Mr. Snotrocket...that is the silliest thing I have ever heard," Mr. Stinkowitz said. "It's obvious that you did not do your reading, or you would know that humans and dinosaurs never co-existed, nor did flatulence have anything to do with the Origin of Man! It's preposterous! You see..."

Mr. Stinkowitz began to lecture all over again. Milo tried to point out that his next class had already started, by the teacher had his eyes shut and couldn't seem to hear a thing as he droned on and on. "Oh well," Milo thought, "Guess this is the rest of my day." He put his head onto his desk again, and let out a soft, sleepy fart that carried him into his next dream...

MORE FUNNY FARTS...

If you laughed really hard at Caveman Farts, I know you'll love these other stinky bestselling books by J.B. O'Neil (for kids of *all* ages!)

http://jjsnip.com/fart-book

And...

http://jjsnip.com/booger-fart-books

Silent but Deadly...As a Ninja Should Be!

http://jjsnip.com/ninja-farts-book

A long time ago, in a galaxy fart, fart away...

http://jjsnip.com/fart-wars

Think twice before you blame the dog!

http://jjsnip.com/dog-farts

And check out my new series, the

Family Avengers!

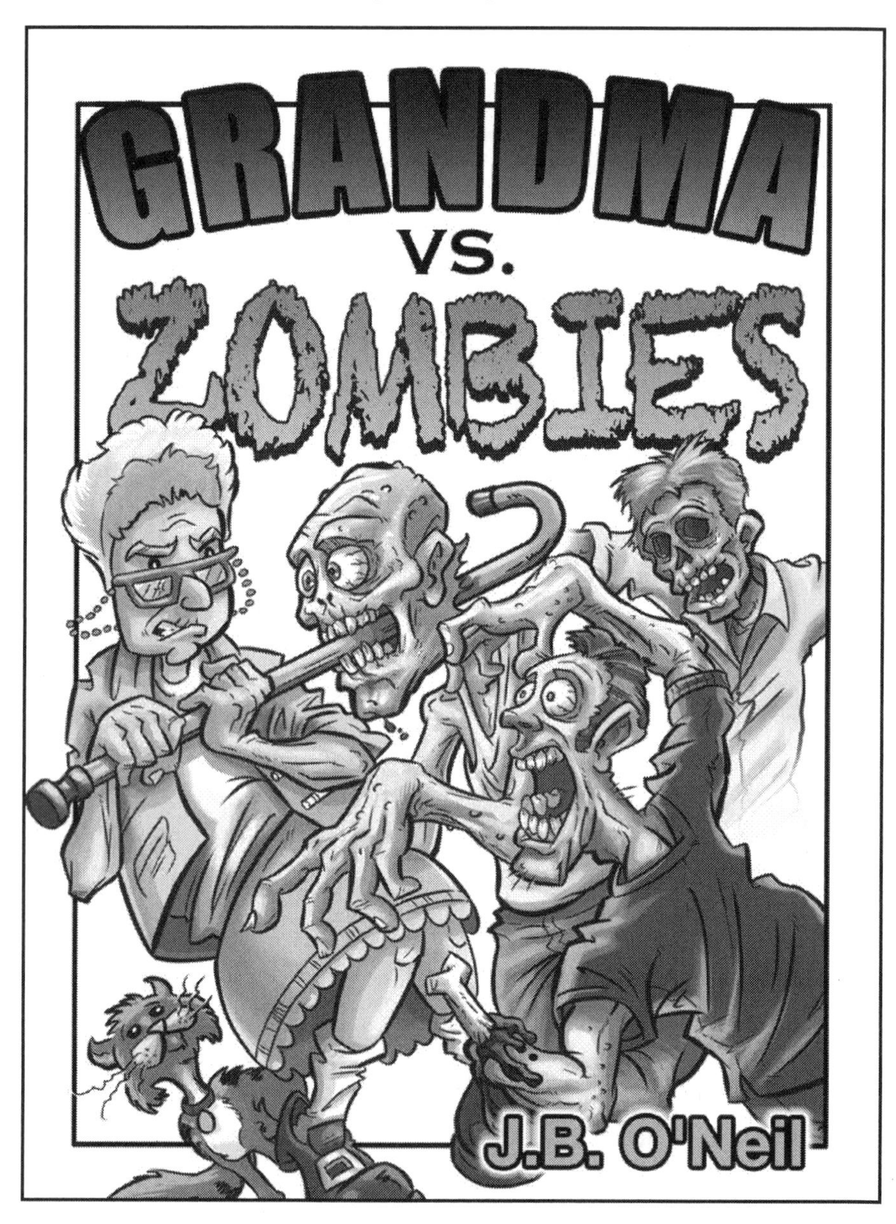

http://jjsnip.com/gvz